Gunilla Wolde

Betsy and the

Random House **New York**

First American Edition, 1976

Printed in Great Britain

Chicken Pox

Betsy's baby brother feels miserable. He has a cough and a runny nose, and he's covered all over with itchy red spots. He is hot and cranky, and he won't stop crying.

Daddy takes his temperature.
It is 101 degrees.
Baby brother has a fever.

Mommy calls the doctor.
She sounds worried.
She asks the doctor
to come over and see
baby brother.

Daddy holds him and
gives him little sips
of juice while Mommy
is on the phone.

When the doctor comes
she is in a great hurry.
She doesn't even stop
to say hello to Betsy.

The doctor examines
baby brother's spots.
She looks in his ears
and down his throat.

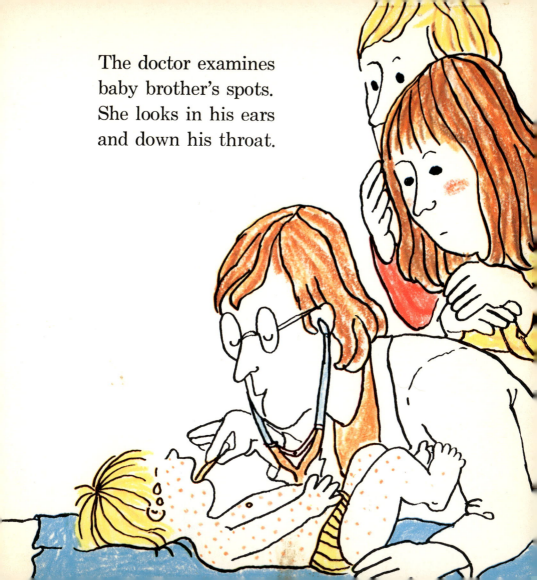

Then she says baby brother
has chicken pox—a disease
that children easily catch.
She writes down the name
of some medicine for
baby brother.

The doctor tells Mommy and Daddy to give
baby brother lots of juice and keep him in bed
until the spots and fever have gone away.
But she doesn't say anything about Betsy.

Betsy feels sorry for her little brother
because he is sick and covered with spots.
But Betsy wishes she had some spots, too.

She looks in the mirror.
There are no spots anywhere—
not even on her tongue.

Betsy decides to paint big red spots
all over herself.

She even paints red spots on her tongue.
Now she looks as if she has chicken pox, too.

Then Betsy goes to show Mommy and Daddy
her chicken pox. But Daddy is rushing off
to the drugstore to get baby brother's
medicine. And Mommy is busy getting his juice
and a clean pair of pajamas. They don't
pay any attention to Betsy.

Mean Daddy!
Horrible Mommy!
Stupid baby brother!
Betsy screams and cries
because nobody cares
how sick *she* is.

Mommy gets angry with Betsy for screaming. Then Daddy gets angry with Mommy for getting angry with Betsy.

But soon everyone calms down.
Daddy goes off to the drugstore.
Mommy and Betsy comfort
each other.
Mommy is just tired
and worried. She
didn't mean to
get angry.

Betsy says she
didn't mean to
get angry
either.

For the rest of the day Betsy, Mommy, and Daddy are busy taking care of baby brother. They have so much to do they forget about Betsy's painted spots.

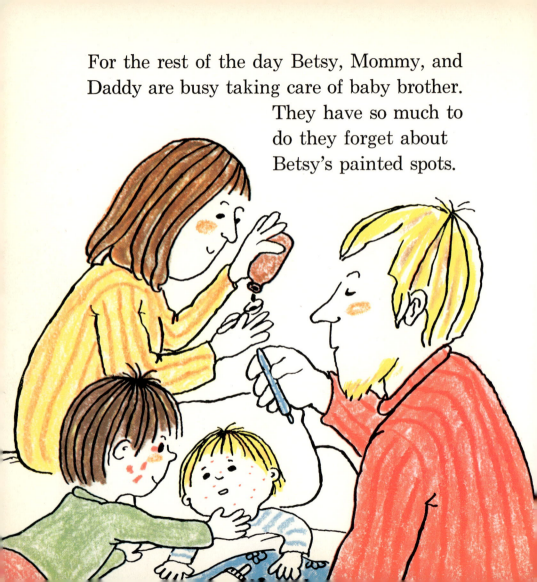

But that evening, while Betsy is getting
ready for bed, something strange happens.
When the *painted* spots are
washed off, Daddy
finds *real* spots
all over Betsy.

Betsy has chicken pox.
She must stay in bed, too, until all
the spots and fever have gone away.
It's funny, but now that Betsy has *real*
chicken pox, she doesn't want them any more.